RAPUNZEL

Written by Saviour Pirotta
Illustrated by Lucy Fleming

There was once a man and a
woman who lived next door to
a witch. The woman was pregnant
and she was always hungry.

Quarto is the authority on a wide range of topics.

Quarto educates, entertains and enriches the lives of our readers—enthusiasts and lovers of hands-on living.

www.quartoknows.com

© 2017 Quarto Publishing plc

This paperback edition first published in 2019 by QED Publishing, an imprint of The Quarto Group. The Old Brewery, 6 Blundell Street, London N7 9BH, United Kingdom. T (0)20 7700 6700 F (0)20 7700 8066 www.QuartoKnows.com

Author: Saviour Pirotta
Illustrator: Lucy Fleming
Designer: Victoria Kimonidou
Editor: Ellie Brough

A catalogue record for this book is available from the British Library.

ISBN 978 1 78603 933 0

Manufactured in Shenzhen, China PP022019

9 8 7 6 5 4 3 2 1

MIX
Paper from responsible sources
FSC® C001701
www.fsc.org

A tasty herb, called rapunzel, grew in the witch's garden.
"I wish I could have some," sighed the woman.

The man didn't want his wife to be hungry so he sneaked
into the witch's garden and stole some rapunzel.

The woman wanted more rapunzel, so the man continued to steal it. Until one night, the witch caught him.

"Let me go," he begged.

"On one condition," cackled the witch.
"You must give me your newborn baby."

In his fear, the poor man
agreed and when the girl was
born, the witch carried her away.

The witch named the girl Rapunzel after the herb.
She locked her up in a tower with no stairs.

As Rapunzel grew, so did her hair, in a long, flowing plait.

When the witch visited Rapunzel, she would call, "Rapunzel, Rapunzel, let down your hair."

Rapunzel would lean out of the window and the witch would climb up, using her plait like a rope.

Rapunzel was lonely and sad.
She would sit by the window
and look at far away towns
and villages, longing to go out.
She sang to pass the time.

Rapunzel didn't know that the
King's son often passed by the tower.
He was so enchanted by her voice
that he longed to meet her.

One day Rapunzel heard
a familiar cry, "Rapunzel,
Rapunzel, let down your hair."

But it was the prince, not the witch, who climbed into the tower.

"I heard you sing and had to meet you," he said. "So I watched from the bushes until I saw how the witch climbed up."

"You must go at once," cried Rapunzel, who had never seen such a beautiful face before. "If the witch finds you, she will hurt you."

"I shall return, my love," promised the prince. "And I shall help you escape."

Every night the prince returned with a handkerchief,
which Rapunzel used to make a rope. She hid it in
a chest, until one day the witch found it.

In an angry rage, she chopped off
Rapunzel's hair and cast a spell,
sending Rapunzel to the desert.

That night the
prince arrived with
another handkerchief.

"Rapunzel, Rapunzel,
let down your hair,"
he cried.

Down came the hair, but
it was the witch waiting
for the prince in the tower.

She put a spell on him too, sending him into the forest.

For months, the prince wandered alone, singing to himself.

"Rapunzel, Rapunzel, let down your hair."

Until one day, finally, Rapunzel replied...

"Is that my prince?"

The prince and Rapunzel found each other at
the point where the forest meets the desert.

Rapunzel and the prince were married and they were never lonely again.

NEXT STEPS

Discussion and Comprehension

Ask the children the following questions and discuss their answers:

· Why did the man sneak into the witch's garden at the start of the book?

· Why do you think that Rapunzel was so lonely?

· How did the Prince plan that Rapunzel could escape?

· How would you try to escape from a tall tower with no stairs?

Learn about Conjunctions

Ask the children to name all the characters in the book and write these on the board. Ask the children who is their favourite character and why. Ask them to form a sentence using the word 'because': 'my favourite character is... because...' Give them lots of examples to support. If able, they can write out their sentences using correct punctuation.

Create a Crown

Give the children a range of card, shiny paper, tissue paper, scissors, glue and coloured pens and ask them to make crowns for the prince and Rapunzel labelled with each name.